Shaun the Sheep MOVIE

THE GREAT ESCAPE

CANDLEWICK
ENTERTAINMENT

First U.S. edition 2015

ISBN 978-0-7636-7738-1

15 16 17 18 19 20 QGT 10 9 8 7 6 5 4 3 2 1

Printed in Taunton, MA, U.S.A.

This book was typeset in Manticore.
The illustrations were created digitally.

Candlewick Entertainment
An imprint of
Candlewick Press
99 Dover Street
Somerville, Massachusetts 02144

www.candlewick.com

CONTENTS

Chapter One
THE CLINK

This is Trumper.

He is the city's animal warden.

He has a perfect record for catching strays.

No one escapes from the Animal Containment Center. No one.

There are all kinds of inmates at the center. There are some tough characters, like the tattooed Rottweiler and the fancy poodle with big muscles.

There are some crazy prisoners, too, like the pit bull terrier. He stares. It's creepy.

But some animals at the center aren't scary at all. Slip, a lonely mutt with a crooked smile, is used to living on the streets. All she wants is a family to call her own.

And the center contains more than just dogs. There's also a tortoise and a sad  goldfish who is very good at playing the harmonica.

There is only one way for inmates to get out: adoption. Trumper doesn't like it, but sometimes visitors come by and choose one of the animals to take home.

When there is a visit, everyone tries to look their best. They primp their fur and bat their eyelashes.

You never know who might be lucky enough to be chosen.

On this day, there is a new captive: a sheep named Shaun! Trumper marches him down the center's main hall and leads him to his cell, where Shaun is surprised to find Mossy Bottom Farm's sheepdog, Bitzer. The pair are the Containment Center's newest inmates.

How on earth did *they* get here?

Chapter Two

FOLLOW THAT CAMPER

Earlier that day, the Flock had been very bad.

Shaun had convinced the other sheep to take a day off. To do this, they needed to fool the Farmer. The sheep jumped over a gate — over and over. The Farmer started to count them, but it made him very sleepy.

The Flock put him to bed in an old camper parked on the farm.

The Farmer was asleep. That could only mean one thing — movie time!

The sheep skipped happily to the farmhouse. They sat down on the

couch, and Shaun handed out bowls

of ice cream. One of the sheep tried

to stick pizza into the toaster.

Another tried to work the remote

control on the TV. Shaun had just

settled onto the couch when . . .

Bitzer walked in. Their day off was over before it had even begun! The disappointed sheep led Bitzer to the camper. He could see the Farmer snoring away inside. It was time to wake him up and get back to work. Bitzer tried the door handle.

It was stuck! He pulled on the handle, rocking the camper.

Bitzer pulled harder. One, two, three . . .

CRUNCH!

The big pull had crushed the log under the camper's wheels. Without the log to hold the camper in place, the whole thing started to roll downhill, out of control. And the Farmer was still inside!

Bitzer ran after the camper, but it was too fast for him to keep up.

It rolled on toward the city, leaving Bitzer panting in its dust.

Eventually, the camper slowed to a stop. The Farmer stepped out of the camper, the door hitting a light pole. The light fixture toppled off the pole and bonked the Farmer on the head. He was knocked out cold.

Bitzer ran over the top of a hill and saw the Farmer, still groggy, being put into an ambulance. The ambulance drove off, and Bitzer kept on running after it.

Chapter Three
CITY SLICKERS

When Bitzer arrived at the hospital, he rushed into the building, but a guard quickly threw him out. *No dogs!*

What could Bitzer do?

Soon after, a man pushed a cart full of laundry through the hospital entrance. The guard didn't see the furry tail sticking out of the cart.

Inside the hospital, Bitzer climbed out of the cart dressed as a doctor. He needed to find the Farmer.

Bitzer walked into an operating room. Uh-oh: everyone in the room thought Bitzer was a surgeon! He did not know what to do. He washed his paws at the sink. Would he have to start cutting the patient?

Bitzer saw a skeleton in the corner. Bones! Bitzer could not help himself. He leaped at the skeleton and locked his teeth around a leg bone.

Clearly, Bitzer was no doctor.

Trumper was called in to catch this stray.

✦❦✦

Meanwhile, the sheep at Mossy Bottom Farm were getting hungry. They needed the Farmer to feed them! They would have to go to the city and find him.

As they rode the bus, they became even hungrier. Where could they find food?

A restaurant!

The sheep dressed up in coats, hats, scarves, and skirts to look like a human family—a very strange human family.

They walked into a fancy restaurant and sat down. The sheep did not know how to act properly. Should they eat the menus?

They watched as a man opened
his menu to read it. They all opened
their menus to read them.

He burped. They burped.

Then Timmy spotted a dessert
cart. Yum!

Luckily, Shaun grabbed Timmy before he was spotted.

*Un*luckily, Shaun did not see that his sweater was caught on the dessert cart! It began to unravel when a waiter pushed the cart.

Soon Shaun was just a naked sheep in a restaurant.

Everyone went bonkers!

Trumper was called in to catch this stray.

Chapter Four
SHEEP RESCUE

Deep inside the Animal Containment Center, Shaun and Bitzer are worried. They need to get the Farmer back to Mossy Bottom Farm. How else will the Flock get food?

Bitzer and Shaun have to escape. But how? No one has ever escaped from here. No one.

They argue. But Shaun and Bitzer don't know that the Flock is trying to rescue them at that very moment.

The Twins are still dressed as a human lady. They walk into the center with their hips swinging.

Trumper thinks this "lady" is very pretty. He hurries over to greet her. Does she want to adopt a pet?

Shaun and Bitzer stare out the window, hoping help will come. Without it, how will they escape? Maybe they are doomed to stay at the Animal Containment Center forever.

 Inside his office, Trumper and the lady are getting friendly. Suddenly, Trumper hears a loud *CRASH!*

The Flock has pulled down the wall, and now Shaun and Bitzer will be free. Hooray!

But the Flock doesn't see Shaun and Bitzer inside. Oh, no — they picked the wrong building!

Inside his cell, Shaun hears the crash and gets an idea. Thinking fast on his hooves, he grabs a piece of chalk.

Bitzer and Shaun hear footsteps. Uh-oh: Trumper is coming.

Trumper runs over and freezes when he sees their cell. There's a big hole in the wall. There's been an escape! Trumper unlocks the door and rushes inside.

SLAM!

Shaun and Bitzer have locked Trumper in their cell! The hole in the wall was only a drawing. They grab Slip from her cell and run outside. They're free!

Chapter Five

HAIR TODAY, GONE TOMORROW

Outside, Shaun, Bitzer, and Slip rejoin the Flock. It is time to find the Farmer.

He's easy to find: he's on a billboard! Using his sheep-shearing skills, he has been working at a hair salon. The Farmer's unique hairstyle has become a hit. He is famous!

But the Farmer has lost his memory. Shaun thinks that the best way to get the Farmer's memory back is to take him home to Mossy Bottom Farm.

That night, the animals return to the hair salon with a plan—and a gate. The sheep put everybody to sleep by jumping the gate, over and over again.

The rescue team grabs the Farmer and puts him on a horse . . .

a fake horse, that is! It is the Flock's getaway vehicle. Now they can leave the city without anyone noticing.

But someone does notice: Trumper!

Trumper isn't fooled by the horse. He knows it must be the escaped convicts! He shoots his electric grabber gun. The claw loops around the horse's legs — shocking Trumper in the process.

The horse drags Trumper along, and they crash through a fence. Soon the horse reaches the camper, and all the animals and the Farmer change vehicles. They use a rope to hitch the camper to a passing bus.

Trumper manages to catch up. He shoots the grabber gun at the

camper and latches on. The camper

moves forward, and the sheep look out.

Oh good, they can't see Trumper

anywhere. Time to head home!

Chapter Six

TRUMPER'S LAST STAND

At Mossy Bottom Farm, the sheep
unload the Farmer from the camper
and wheel him toward the farmhouse. But in the distance they see
something. Oh, no, it's Trumper!
He's followed them to the farm!

The animals take the sleeping
Farmer and hide in the shed.

But Trumper doesn't try to get in. Instead, he climbs into the tractor. Then he drives the tractor right at the shed — and pushes it toward the quarry!

The shed is pushed along until it slams into a wire fence. The Flock tries to wake the Farmer — they need his help! Quickly, they grab some manure and hold it under his nose. It works, all right!

The Farmer is confused — who are these animals? Where is he? He spots an old photo on the wall.

It shows Bitzer, Shaun, and the rest of the Flock gathered around the Farmer.

Suddenly something falls into place. The Farmer remembers! He bursts through the shed door, ready to save the day . . . and drops down into the quarry!

Luckily, his foot gets caught.
The sheep lower Bitzer down to
rescue the Farmer, while Shaun
climbs across the tractor to take
on Trumper.

Shaun and Trumper struggle.
Trumper falls out of the tractor,
and his pants rip to reveal his red
underpants. Someone
else sees the
under-
pants,
too:
a big
bull!

The bull slams into Trumper, sending him sailing up into the air. He lands in a huge pile of manure.

Hooray! Now everything can go back to normal.

Back at the farmhouse, the pigs have made a mess. Food and pig poop are everywhere! When they see the Farmer returning, the pigs try to clean up, fast!

One pig quickly washes the dishes. Another needs to get rid of a big bowl of popcorn, so he eats it.

The last pig to leave the farmhouse carefully wipes the door handle.

He doesn't want to leave any prints.
The pigs scurry away.

Thanks to Shaun and Bitzer's great escape, Trumper is fired and the Containment Center is renamed the Adoption Center.

Mossy Bottom Farm goes back to its regular routine. Shaun's day off was a great adventure!